# The House on Maple Ave.

by

Candace Nadine Breen

**iSBN:** 9798846887657

Independently published



Printed in the United States of America.

DEDICATION

*For all those who want to fly!*

*Spread your wings and fly above the clouds!*

*There are no limits.*

We used to walk by every day after school. The windows were always dark, and the lawn was overgrown with grass and weeds. The grownups said that no one lived in that old decrypt house because it was so unkempt, but one day my friends and I were coming home from the neighborhood playground and saw otherwise.

There, amidst the overgrowth of the front lawn, stood a girl about our age. Her face was gray like ash and her hair hung in limp strands about her head. She wore a plaid jumper skirt, a dingy white, long-sleeved blouse. Her eyes were wide and expressionless. We stopped on our bikes and waved at her.

"Hey, how're you doing? Do you live there? Are you new here?" She continued to look at us with wide, vacant eyes that were encircled with blackness. Her lips did not move, she said nothing.

"Well, I'm John and this is Paul, and that's Jared. We live in the neighborhood. Wanna go with us to the playground some time? You can borrow my bike if you don't have one." I said. Still no response.

“Okay, see you ‘round.” We rode our bikes away, and the girl slowly turned her head in our departing direction.

Later that afternoon, as my friends and I were talking on the playground about the strange girl, Jared said that his old sister once told him a story about a girl who died in that house a long time ago.

“And they said she just died,” Jared's conspiratory whispered. “She just died in the house! She was really sick and her skin was pale and back then they didn’t have medicines and stuff so she just died. I don’t know where she’s buried, but my sister says her spirit sometimes shows up at that creepy ole house on Maple and just stands there.

“So you’re saying we saw a ghost and not a real live girl?” I asked.

“I’m just sayin’ what my sister said.” Jared answered, lowering his eyes.

The next day, we went to Maple Ave again to see if the girl was standing outside the house. I didn't believe in ghosts, but Jared was sold. I wasn't sure about Paul,though whose face wore no expression.

I intended to go right into the yard. We saw her. She was standing in the same place. This time, she was sitting on an old rickety swing that was tied to a tree in the front yard. She didn't speak when I waved.

"Hi", I said. She just stared at me with glassy eyes. The other boys tried to tell me not to go inside the yard. I opened the gate, its rickety squeak alerting the girl of my presence. The girl stopped swinging and turned towards me. She stared at me as I got closer to her.

"Hey you wanna come with us to the playground?" She said nothing. I touched her shoulder and quickly withdrew my hand in shock. She was ice cold despite her clothing.

"Well, if you wanna sometime, you could come join us," I said. I backed out of the yard, feeling goosebumps suddenly covering my entire body.

When we were at the playground with our bikes, I told the boys how cold the girl felt when I touched her.

Jared said, "Told ya! She ain't not among the living," he added with a mysteriously sounding whisper in my face. I pushed him away.

"So you're saying I touched a ghost?" I said with increasingly vanishing disbelief.

"You touched a dead person!" Jared said.

Pete said, "You know you should just stop going by there and talking to her. She obviously ain't interested, and *then* you went and *touched* her!"

That night, as I slept, I tossed and turned. I couldn't get that girl's face out of my mind. It was like she was haunting my brain!

My window blew open, blanketing my bedroom in the cool night air. I sat up in bed and made a move to shut the window, but hesitated. Suddenly, there was the girl standing at the foot of my bed, looking at me with those expressionless eyes. Both startled and frightened, I scrunched up against my headboard.

"What do you want?" I whimpered, bed sheets up to my chin.

"Your soooooulllll," the girl said, her mouth an endless black hole.

*At least she finally talked,* I thought. She stretched out a hand towards me and seemed to float in the air right where she was standing.

"I want your soooouuuuul," she said, again. I yelled for my parents, but no one came.

“It’s been a looooong time since I have eaten. I am huuuuuunnnnngry,” she said.

“If you’re hungry,” I shouted in defiance.” There are some cookies downstairs!”

“I don’t nced that food. I need your soooooouuuuul!”

“Why do you need my soul?” The girl laughed and her laugh echoed throughout my room. I screamed. Instantly, there was the sound of footsteps coming up the stairs. My door smashed open and my parents were standing next to my bed.

“Are you all right, John?” my mom asked, wrapping her arms around me. I pointed to the foot of my bed, but the girl was no longer there.

“She *was* there!” I cried, burying my head into my mother’s mom.

“Who?” my dad said.

“The girl at the house on Maple Ave!” My parents looked at each other knowingly. They knew something they weren’t telling me. My mother walked over to the window and closed it.

"John, you need to stop going by that house," my mom said, a serious look on her face." A girl died in that and her spirit lives there. She tries to come back to the world of the living and anyone she catches, she takes their soul so she can live again. Stay away from that house."

"But Mom, I touched her, and she felt real!"

"You *touched* her?" My mother's eyes were suddenly wide with astonishment.

"I just touched her shoulder, and she was cold."

"You touched her," my father said. "Now she's going to keep coming back for your soul. We have to stop her. We have to make sure her ghost is gone for good." My mother nodded in agreement.

"John, I want you to do something and we must do it tonight while the moon is still full," my mother said.

My parents took me to the attic. I've never been in the attic. My father pulled out a big heavy box, opened it. My mother pulled a mason jar from the box while my father grabbed two seven-day candles: one red and one white.

They led me to the kitchen where my mother poured the thick red muddy-looking liquid from the mason jar into a tall glass of milk that she warmed in the microwave.

"Drink this—" she held out the glass to me.

"Um, mom—-"

"*All* of it." she said, firmly. I drank.

"Yuck, what is this?"

"She will return every night until she gains your soul. This will mix with your blood so that when she reaches inside your body for your soul, she will be poisoned."

"The milk is for you, to keep you in a sleepy state," my father added.

"What's in this stuff?" I asked, again.

"That is not important. You just finish all of it." So I did.

"You will soon feel tired," my mom said. "That is to trick her into thinking you are an easy target and that taking your soul will be easy.

"The red candles represent blood and are to draw her in. The white candle is to banish her from our world by summoning and attracting the gatekeeper spirits who will take her back to her soul where it resides in the world of the undead where she can no longer bypass the light and enter our world to feed off the souls of the living.

"How do you know all of this?" I asked.

"Your mother and I were kids once, too, in this town. That girl was deathly sick and died in that house when you grandma was a kid," my father answered.

As my eyelids drooped, my mother explained that after my Mima got married, she gave birth to my mother and later my aunts and uncles , she made a jar of that stuff because people spoke of the girl returning. Kids were suddenly disappearing and my Mima knew she had to teach her children how to make the liquid and always keep it in a mason jar in a nice, dry place in their homes.

"Appalachian magick," my mom called it. My Mima was a witch who practiced a lot of Appalachian magick before she moved here to the valley after her husband, my Papi, transitioned. She said that she was getting too old for the mountains.

For the rest of the night, sleep wasn't as restless as I thought it would be. I went back to bed knowing that something was going to happen that night. Would she return on the same night? I guess she would keep coming until she got my soul, no matter how many tries that took her.

Although I dozed off and on in my bed, I could not fall completely asleep. I stared at the two lit candles my father had placed at my bedside. The house was so eerily quiet. My parents had said that they would camp outside my bedroom door just in case things didn't go well. They had blankets and pillows strewn in the hallway outside my bedroom, and I could hear my father's loud snoring. I really didn't want to see the girl again. I was afraid. Unfortunately, my eyes slowly closed in slumber.

*"Heeeelllleeennn!"* a scratchy voice awakened me.

*"My name is Heelleenn!"* It was the girl floating at the foot of my bed, her eyes now as dark and round as her abysmal mouth.

*"Tonight, I will have your sooooouuuuuullllll!"* I shivered and braced for the impact of her hand being thrust through my chest. Frozen with fear, I sat up in bed.

"Then, come get it, Helen!" I said between clenched teeth, feigning bravery. My words seemed to anger her and she let out an ear-piercing scream. She waved an arm towards my bedroom door and I heard it lock. I could hear my parents banging on the door and jiggling the handle to no avail. I was trapped inside of my bedroom with Helen, who wanted my soul. My only consolation was knowing she'd be poisoned as soon as she reached into my body–at least, I hoped she would.

Helen flew towards me, an icy wind trailing behind her like the train of a wedding gown. She screamed again in my face, her frigid breath smelling of death and decay. I turned my head in disgust as a pain shot through my chest. She had shoved her hand into the depths of my body in order to retrieve my soul, which she so desperately wanted.. When she withdrew her arm, her once dingy white sleeve was covered in blood–my blood. Again, she reached into my chest, this time screaming as though she had been stabbed. She looked at me in utter disgust. Astonishment and fear colored her ghoulish face. A line of red liquid rushed up her boney fingers, arms and neck. Her hollow eyes narrowed.

*"You tricckked meeeee, you bad, bad boy!"* she screamed into my face. Just as she drew back her arm, exposing sharp claws, another blast of wind blew open my bedroom window. With blurred vision, I could make out the appearance of several figures bathed in blinding white robes ascending upon the girl who had now become so agitated that she growled and clawed at my bedpost. She was being grabbed and dragged away from my bed towards the open window. She emitted the most unearthly sounds until finally, the air was sucked out of my room, closing the window and popping open my bedroom door. My parents fell into the room crying and throwing their arms around me. Before I closed my eyes from sheer exhaustion, I saw the white candle go out, followed by an unnoticed shattering of the candle in the red glass jar. Millions of glass shards remained atop my bureau.

Helen was gone, and I was safe.

# ABOUT THE AUTHOR

Author, artist, and mystic Dr. Candace Nadine Breen is an author with a unique background which manifests through her writings  Dr. Breen is a former Providence Public Schools teacher and has written many books that she will be more than happy to autograph and discuss. She began writing and illustrating her own stories on looseleaf paper when she was in third grade with her first unpublished work "Down on the Farm" which reflected Candace's paternal family's  Southern agricultural influence. Her stories caught on in school and she continued furiously writing stories that often depicted her classmates in fantasy settings and, eventually. She has published poetry books after falling in love with the art of the way imagery tells a story through poetry.

Years later, Candace found she could also write memoirs, short fantasy and sci-fi books as well as children's books and she dove into all of them becoming a self-published author!

In "Today, I Feel Ugly," "Born Different," and "After the Darkness," Dr. Breen shares her stories of abandonment and abuse, and how she learned to use her experiences and unique gifts to live a happy, fulfilling life.

Her children's books "The Rainbow Ribbon" and "Moon Child", and "Cuddly Cat" teach children of all ages valuable lessons of community and self-discovery.

Candace also has a number of sci-fi and paranormal short stories including "Unforgiven", "Ungrateful", "Taton House", and "Zanobie Foretold: Book1".

Candace holds a B.A. in Secondary Education/English, a M.A. in Human Services/Marriage and Family, and a M.S. in Metaphysics and a Doctorate in

Metaphysics. She resides in Barrington with her devoted husband, two very talented and creative children, and their two loving and mystical cats.

Visit Candace's author website to learn more about her work at candacenadinebreen.com

www.ingramcontent.com/pod-product-compliance
Lightning Source LLC
LaVergne TN
LVHW091244150826
845673LV00003B/1296

* 9 7 9 8 8 4 6 8 8 7 6 5 7 *